I0624329

Maroon Medicine

Maroon Medicine

E.A. Dodd

MINT EDITIONS

Maroon Medicine was first published in 1905.

This edition published by Mint Editions 2021.

ISBN 9781513211961 | E-ISBN 9781513210766

Published by Mint Editions®

 MINT
EDITIONS

minteditionbooks.com

Publishing Director: Jennifer Newens
Design & Production: Rachel Lopez Metzger
Project Manager: Micaela Clark
Typesetting: Westchester Publishing Services

Contents

PREFACE

In the four short stories that are now set forth to the Public,—I have in no way touched upon the Social Problems I might say Problem,— which, as a rule, engross the attention of writers who deal with life in Tropical Countries. On the contrary, I have avoided all such deep questions, and have attempted merely to portray the lighter and more pleasant side of the labouring class in the hills. The stories, indeed, are scarcely more than sketches, but sketches, from life, and as such may have some value.

I have tried to instil into this little book, the spirit, so gay and careless of the people I have encountered, and their simple cuteness. Mr. Watson, however, is hardly an ordinary type, and has been made up from two or three characters. Some people may object to the two love letters in the story, "The Courting of the Dudes," as being too well expressed and civilized, but it may be remarked that they were composed very much after the manner and matter of two or three letters that had been actually written and which I had the good fortune to read.

E.A. Dodd,
Jamaica

MAROON MEDICINE

I t was just one of the cottages that you see scattered all over Jamaica; possessing four walls made of plaster and lathes, and a thatched roof—the whole enclosing two rooms, dignified by the names, of bed-room and hall. From one corner stretched a small barbecue, which again at one corner fed a small, "Kick-um-buck" tank, covered over with rough logs to prevent people falling in. All around, for the space of about half an acre, grew in picturesque medley, coffee bushes, yams, breadfruit trees, orange trees, the products of the lower mountains in the Parish of Manchester. A couple of fowls scratched around the house, and a hungry-looking pig messed about his little railed in pen.

It had rained in the night, but the morning had broken exceeding fresh and fair, warm yet cool, with a bright beauty that I cannot believe could have been surpassed anywhere. It may be that the pig felt something of this, or it may be that he knew that his morning meal was nearly ready, but undoubtedly he felt happy and showed it in little unmusical squeals. His master sat at the edge of the barbecue, chopping up into a box with his cutlass, steadily and with attention, a few small canes. Having finished chopping all except one choice bit which he reserved for his own consumption, he rose and went to the pen, where he put the box before the pig. He then proceeded to chew his own piece of cane, with a certain amount of intelligent repose on his face.

This face of his was long and of a neutral brown, with the bony chin going in sharply up to the neck. The man had a wide and mobile mouth, with a quaint twitch at one side, two small twinkling eyes and a bald and sloping forehead under his hat of plaited thatch.

It was a perfect morning in the end of November, yet to judge from the slight frown which crept up and marred the repose of Mr. Watson's face, one could not think the latter was in sympathy with nature's peace. The reason was simple, Mr. Watson had very little ready money; and Christmas was coming, and he felt aggrieved with himself and his wits, which were not in the habit of failing him. His thoughts ran in this groove:

"An a what me got fe Chris'mas bar dis little maugre pig? Me cawfee no sell well, and me premento don bear, a what me got? Me we have to do sompin?"

His musing was suddenly interrupted by the approach of a neighbour, who was walking through to his ground, and who stopped to salute him.

"Hi, mornin' Miser Watson!"

"Mornin', Coz! How you do?"

"So, so, sah, a not too well an' a not too bad, you a feed you pig, sah"

Mr. Watson turned carelessly and twitched the few scraggy hairs that formed his whiskers, with a gesture peculiar to him.

"Yes, sah, me a feed him, but a wha de use? I buy him back dis tree weeks from Miser White at James Hall, and I gie'm yam pealin! cocoa head, banana an' all sort o' ting, an look pon him now, h'no ah piece fatter than when I buy him. Well (with emphasis) as you might seh, a doan pay much fe him, but it tan like a not goin get no more fe him."

"Hi, but a wha do de pig den?" said the neighbour sympathetically. "Him really ought fe fat. Aldo some of dem, a so dey tan. I remember dis man Joe Crawford got a pig; well when he buy him, h' not too fat so h'n get plenty o feedin', cane, cocoa head an' I don know what; an' him feed that pig fe true, but you believe me sah, dat pig was no fatter at de end of tree monts dan when he got him fus' time. Mus a same way wid dis."

Mr. Watson looked with a philosophical calm at the pig.

"Well, it may be. Ah same way wid some man; you wi see some o' dem eat, eat, an eat and yet dem never get fat, dey tin all de time."

"You speak true, sah, a same way wi some men."

After a pause the neighbour hitched his bankra better on his shoulder and said:

"Yes, sah, ah jus' a walk trew to me groun' go look somepin for me wife."

"You welcome, you welcome," said Mr. Watson hospitably, "a no hear you wife sick? a fe true?"

"Yes sah. It true! night before las' she tek in wid a single pain in de stomach, De pain hol' her dat way. Well she go to bed, an' ah tek dis bush dem call "Piobba" and a bwoil it down and mek some tea, gie 'er but it doan any good, den ah mek some oder tea out o'dis other bush; "Vervain," an' gie 'er dat, but dat also doan do any good; and all dis time de pain dat bad. Well yesterday about sun hot, Mrs. Weekly advise me try some soda and nut oil mix wid a little water and I do so, and since then she feel a little better and could walk bout de yard in the evenin'. Yes sah she really sick but she not too bad dis morning."

During this speech Mr. Watson showed his sympathy in a few well chosen sounds and affirmatives which cannot be reproduced by any combination of letters.

"Ah glad fe hear she better. Some of dese teas is really wonaful. To be sure some doctors good. I woan seh dey not, but mos' time you go to dem, you jus' wase you money. Dis bush or dat is all I want."

"You right, Miser Watson, you quite right," agreed the other heartily, "Some doctors no wut a grass louse, aldo dis Doctor Pratt him really good." Then moving on, "Well ah gone, Miser Watson."

"Yes, sah. Mr. Watson sent him on his journey with a wave of his hand and then resumed the reflective chewing of his cane. I may remark here that the man's ground was five miles away, but there is nothing strange in this; for the Jamaica Peasant will travel up to ten or twelve miles to get some fresh piece of land to till and work as a ground. Every two or three years he throws up one piece and takes another fresh bit.

After his friend's departure Mr. Watson's face took on an even more reflective look; and for half an hour he lolled in deepest thought; then straightening with a brightened face, he walked into his house, and emerged with his jacket on, having been without it before.

His face now was the calm inscrutable and cunning face of Mr. George Watson of Every Garden. This was the name of his place, but how it had arisen, and what was its origin, Mr. Watson himself did not know.

He left the house and yard now in charge of a little ragged girl, his daughter, and took one of those paths, which fed the main road like tributaries of a river. Coming out on this, he walked for about three miles, when he came into a village, consisting of two or three rival shops which sold various, assorted articles, from very weak rum to a drawing book, and a couple of professional houses of shoemakers and blacksmith. At one of the former he bought a sixpence worth of soda, and between the three, two dozen pint bottles, saying in sort of excuse that Mrs. Smith (who made bread) had asked him to buy the former for her, and as regards the latter, he was speculating in bottles, and was going to sell to a man from Kingston. He also gave out that he was going up to the Mile Gully Mountains to invest in ginger.

Having bought what he wanted, and having refreshed his mind with a little light conversation, he left and went home where he was busy all day mixing in the privacy of his half-tumbled down kitchen, some vile-looking stuff.

It was perhaps between four and five next morning when Mr. Watson started for the Mile Gully Mountains "to invest in Ginger," driving his donkey, yclept Alice, before him. The hampers contained the two dozen bottles he had bought the day before, a dozen on either side, empty no longer—also some little provision for his journey—a gill bammy, a little pork already boiled, some yams and some oranges. His house he had locked up, but the pig and the cultivation around he had left on the charge of his neighbour and daughter. This latter by the way being driven from under the paternal roof, had taken up her abode for the time being with her aunt (?) She was not Mr. Watson's only child, having three brothers and a sister alive. These, however, having come to the conclusion that their father was not perfect, in his ideas regarding obedience in his children, had severally run away to other yards, a common enough practice in Jamaica. Needless to say, Mr. Watson did not go after them. His was a philosophical soul and he in no way regretted not having to feed three hungry children. He would not have received them back; and his children knew it.

By the time the sun had risen and another perfect day had begun, Mr. Watson had passed Mandeville and was nearing Williamsfield. On reaching the latter place, he stopped near the Railway Station under the shade of an overhanging roof of a front house, and sitting down proceeded to assuage his hunger with half the bammy, half the pork, and half the oranges. The yam was destined to be roasted and eaten higher up when he had come to the end of his journey.

After half an hour's rest, Mr. Watson rose, stretched himself, and started again with a touch and a word to Alice.

From here onwards his road led higher and higher, and at about mid day he entered the district he was bound for. At one or two houses near the road, he enquired his way to the yard of Mr. Hezekiah Brooks. This Brooks had once travelled his way and had partaken of Mr. Watson's hospitality, the latter putting him up for a couple of days. He undoubtedly would now in his turn be glad to put up his former host. After about half an hour's walk, Mr. Watson came to the Brooks yard and found the gentleman of the house at home, who welcomed him and expressed his delight at seeing him again. Mr. Brooks was a small brown man, a carpenter by trade, of not much force of character, yet kindly and good-natured.

"Ah really glad fe see you, Miser Watson. Don mention it, sah. Jus' tie you donkey to dat tree and sted dis way. Me no ha much as regards house and place to sleep ina, but weh me hav, you welcome to."

Over some roasted yam and boiled saltfish the little man took upon himself to find out why Mr. Watson had come up that way.

"Excuse me, sah, and I doan mean nutten by it, but ah curious to know whey you travel dis way fur. You mus' be going buy and speculate?"

Mr. Watson resting easily against the side of the kitchen twitched his whisker:

"Well you guess right enough, Miser Brooks, I am goin' fe speculate, Ah did notice dat our way, well dem doan grow ginger or nutten to speak of, an' de backra ladies dem, dey always a want ginger. So I tink if I buy some up dis way an' tek it down, a might a mek a little pon me bargin." Mr. Brooks looked at him.

"Yes, sah, you might a really mek sompting pon it. Me neber tink o' dat, or me might ah try it before. You mus' be going carry it, de ginger in a bottle, me notice you got plenty o'bottle."

Mr. Watson ate his saltfish and remarked indifferently:

"Oh de bottle only got a little Maroon Medicine in dem. It such a good thing for sickness dat I tink dat as a coming up here wey dey doan know it and colds is plenty ah could ah sell a little here or dere."

Mr. Brooks got so interested that he stopped eating.

"Weh you call it, sah, Maroon Medicine? Me no hear 'bout it before. A wah it good for?"

Mr. Watson took a bite out of his roast yam.

"Well, down our side, dey use it for all sort o' sickness, but specially for boile, and stomach ache and cold wid fever. A see plenty o' people cure wid it."

"Me would a really like fe try it"; said Mr. Brooks. "Me daughter, Susan yah, often trouble wid stomach ache. How you sell it sah?"

"Well, as it mek out a somptin' dear enough, me sell it at shilling a bottle, but as you is a fren' a would a gie it to you for sixpence."

"But it's really good, Miser Watson?" asked Mr. Brooks.

"Well it is not for me to praise me own ting, aldo in dis case it really not mine, for I didn't mek it, a Maroon mek it for me, but of all de medicine and fever bush I know, none cure you so quick as dis. But of course if you doan want it, well den doan buy it."

Mr. Brooks hastened to assure his friend that he meant nothing by his remark.

"A only want fe know, Miser Watson, and me tink me wi tek a bottle, sah."

Mr. Watson sold a bottle to Mr. Brooks and the latter promptly made Susan take a small dose, which undoubtedly had a certain medicinal effect by night.

Towards five o'clock in the afternoon the two men took their way to the popular rumshop in the neighbourhood, Mr. Watson wisely leaving all medicine behind, trusting to Mr. Brooks to advertise him. The little man was of a loquacious turn of mind and that evening certainly lived up to Mr. Watson's trust. Over a glass of weak rum and water he told in graphic terms how he had given Susan one dose not two hours ago, and already.

"It hab a wonaful affeck!"

Mr. Watson when questioned about it gave polite but modest answers, only asserting that he had got an old Maroon to make it up for him, the latter assuring him that they used it a lot among his people and he, Mr. Watson, had indeed found it good. Towards half past seven Mr. Brooks and his guest returned home where they found Susan emitting groans at intervals and rather sick. Mr. Watson comforted her and her father by assuring them that she would feel much better by morning and that the medicine always made one feel sick at first.

Next morning Susan was much better and radiant at having taken such a "wonaful" medicine. She had no pain and said she had a great appetite. Her father was delighted and Mr. Watson felt cheerful himself, having had up to now certain doubts about the after effects of his medicine. He sold six bottles that day, taking over ginger and home made ropes in part payment, where the buyer did not have sufficient cash. They went out again to the shop in the evening, and Mr. Watson found himself being rapidly advertised. He was asked several times how it was made and what of, but he refused to tell saying that he had promised the Maroon not to. Various guesses were made at its composition which produced a desire in every person to taste it, and by the end of a week Mr. Watson had sold every bottle, and he found himself regretting he had not brought more with him. Most of the people who had taken it felt much better for having done so. Making the most of his job, he loaded his donkey once more and started for home, giving out that he was going for more medicine which he would sell more cheaply this time. He reached home after another half day's travelling and found after selling his ginger etc., he had realized one pound five shillings on his adventure. Not being satisfied he made more medicine, and after Christmas sold to an appreciative market on the Mile Gully Mountains.

In conclusion I should say that soon after Mr. Watson had left the Mile Gully district the second time, some slanderous and evil reports got abroad about him, and the numerous buyers of his "Maroon Medicine" were heard to say that "dey wish dey could a catch dat—man agen, dey would a gie him medicine fe true!"

Paccy Rum

I t was about 3 o'clock in the afternoon—the hour when the sun seems brightest and hottest in the tropics. Along the heavy grey sand of the beach were ranged a number of black canoes, some high up from the sea,—these had come in from early morning—others which had just been beached still on the wet shore. On the horizon, the sails of a few late fishing boats could just be seen appearing on their way back from their fish pots. They would reach White Bay, as the bend in the shore was called, in about an hour's time. The gunnels of the boats which had last come in, were thickly lined with women and girls, buying fish from the fishermen, and making a loud clamour over the business. The atmosphere about was heavy with the strong raw smell of fish, in all states, live fish, dead fish, fish boiling, fish roasting, and fish being cleaned. The sea was dazzling with a thousand lights, glittering on the moving wave tops, especially in the west and more directly under the sun; out in the South-east and far away under the low lying and purple hills, it was a rich blue, and nearer, but in the same direction, a tender green. From the bay and following the shore was a long line of cocoanut palms bending over towards the water and looking top-heavy, with their heavy masses of boughs Separated from these and so near the canoes which were selling fish, that the rush of the foam almost reached the roots, were a couple of palms affording at their curved bases seats which were generally occupied. Under the shade of one of these palms a middle sized man with a long bony face and small eyes and large "weh-fe-do" hat, was barganing with a woman for two small mullet. The woman had bought a string of fish—of which the mullet formed a part, for sixpence a few hours ago, and was now trying to get the man to pay "quatty" or penny-half-penny for about the eighth part.

"Oh, but Miser Watson, you can see dem wut quatty! dem wut more if it come to dat, but sake ah you, you can tek dem fe quatty!"

Mr. Watson slowly stroked his whiskers and wrinkled up his eyes to shut out the glare which was on the sea.

"Well, Miss Jane, you seh dem wut quatty, and I tink dem wut gill, and if dats what you goin ask all de time fe dem, ah wi hav to guh look elsewhere."

The woman looked at the fish and at Mr. Watson's face undecidedly, then bending over her tray:

"Mek ah tie up me fish den, you want too much fe you money, sah!"

Mr. Watson shouldered his "bankra" and turned to go with such final decision in his movement that it made the woman say hurriedly:— "Alright, Miser Watson, see you fish yah! Mr. Watson turned and putting down his "bankra," took the fish calmly and gave the woman her gill, which she received with a deep sigh, that would have deceived no one:

"Lard but it cheap! Dem tek advantage of a poor ooman!"

Putting up the fish carefully, Mr. Watson shouldered his bankra again and turned away with a "well ah gone, Miss Jane," to which the woman accorded a gracious "yes sah!" in a tone of voice whose kindliness one did not expect from her former bargaining.

Quitting the canoes and people Mr. Watson walked a little way up the beach, then turned at right angles on his left, up a path which after a minute, brought him out on the main road. For about a mile he walked along inland when, coming round a bend in the road, he entered a small village. Though small, it was, however, of some importance as one could easily see, for it had a Market, a Post Office and a Police Station. Through the gate of the Station Yard he turned in and walked up to a Constable who was sitting in shirt sleeves on the piazza of the house. The station with its yard, like all other Police Stations in the Island, was scrupulously clean and well-kept; and there was the usual air of neatness and respectability about the whole that spoke well for the discipline of "the Force."

"You come back quick!" said the constable to Mr. Watson as the latter approached him.

"Yes sah, me nuh top no time down ah de beach. Ah jus buy me two little fish dem an come back fe me bundle and donkey to start fe de mountin."

"Well see you bundle deh!" said the constable pointing to a corner in the piazza where a shallow open box lay filled to overflowing with coloured cloths, handkerchiefs, etc., and bound round with a thatch rope. Mr. Watson entered the piazza and putting down the bankra, untied the rope and proceeded to pack the upper clothes more neatly. Having arranged them, he put a piece of oil skin over all and strapped the whole again.

"What you going do wid dem stuff?" asked the constable with a smile, as Mr. Watson finished his repacking. Mr. Watson turned and looked thoughtfully at the constable:

"Well, sah, ah doan know what ah goin do wid dem rightly. Ah may keep dem, ah may sell dem, well den of course you wun know bout dat," here the constable laughed and said "you speak true, I wun know bout dat."

"Because, proceeded Mr. Watson gravely," ah no got no license, but to tell you de troot, corporal, ah doan know rightly what ah goin do wid dem."

"Well ah doan tink I wi know me-self, bar you tell me!" answered the Constable who was not a Corporal by the way, but just an ordinary policeman.

"Oh I wi tell you alright, when ah come down agen!" answered Mr. Watson as he lifted his box out to where a donkey was tied under a lignumvitæ tree. He strapped, or rather roped the box on the donkey's back, which also bore the burden of two hampers, then came back for his bankra.

"Ah no hear that some man or other did da sell rum widout a license up your way?" said the constable, as Mr. Watson gathered up his guiding rope and prepared to start:

Mr. Watson rubbed the side of his face slowly, and answered as if in deep thought. "Now you remin' me corporal; ah did hear bout it, not up my way to be sure, but down ah Mary Town. But I neber hab anyting to do wid such wickedness, so ah carn tell you fe true as I neber come into contack wid dem. Well, ah goin, corporal! he added as the Constable did not say anything more.

"Yes sah" answered the Policeman with a grunt.

Giving the donkey a fillip with the rope, Mr. Watson started and was soon out of sight of the village and on the road leading up to the hills where his home lay. Shortly after he had left the station yard, the Constable with whom he had been talking, wont into an inner room of the station house and remarked to the real Corporal who was sitting at a desk writing.

"Him no got any rum this time, Corporal! I did really tink me'd ah catch him." The Corporal turned round, "I did tink so meself. Did you look in his box properly?" The Constable nodded "well, Corporal, ah raise up all de clort dem and ah see no sign of it. But you tink a man would ah leave his box wid rum slap ina de station piazza? Him no fool!"

"Fac! It is a fac!" answered the Corporal musingly. "Him mus' ah hear dat we are on the look out and tek warning; nex' time ah goin search him properly doh."

"You right, Corporal!" answered the other, "Him wi sure got some dat time. But, Lard him cunning sah."

Meanwhile, Mr. Watson, not entirely unconscious that he was being talked about, was wending his way slowly up the steep beginning of a long hill. By sunset he had got over the more arduous and bigger part of his journey, and by about eight or nine o'clock he entered his own yard. He unloaded the donkey and gave her over to the charge of his daughter, a girl of about fifteen years, who, taking her, gave her drink and tied her out in a grassy patch. Mr. Watson put up everything carefully, taking a special care over six large quart bottles which he had found wrapped up in some clothes at the bottom of the box. The very boldness of his action in leaving his box with six bottles of rum at the station had brought him safely through the hands of the police. Then he went to bed after a hot dinner of bread-kind and salt fish.

During the earlier part of the next day Mr. Watson took it easy, resting doubtless after the weary journey of yesterday. Towards the latter part of the afternoon, however, he went out to the village of Beersheba which was near his place, and stayed there two or three hours. He seemed to have gone there with some purpose, for next day he had plenty of visitors, who first examined his cloth and handkerchiefs, then bought according to their liking. He also managed to exchange his six quart bottles for silver coin at a price double what he paid for them. By evening he had got rid of all his cloth and stuffs and was plainly satisfied with the results of his undertaking. "Dem Constable ah watch me fe true, Lorita" said he to his daughter in the privacy of their kitchen as he sat smoking his dirty-looking clay pipe.

"Dem search you box no sah?" answered Lorita with eager interest stopping for a minute in her work of pealing some sweet potatoes.

"Yes chile! Dem raise up all de elort dem at de side wen ah down at de Bay. Dem neber really look clean true it, because dem neber dream dat ah would ah leave rum slap ina de station, but dem look in a dey." Lorita laughed out loud with the noisy into nation peculiar to her race, and said:

"Lard but you fool dem sah!" Mr. Watson even permitted a feeble sort of grin to pass over his face which showed he was very much pleased with himself, for he never went so far as to laugh and seldom to smile. "Wen you going down agen sah?" asked Lorita after a pause.

"Tree week from yesterday to come." answered her father. "But ah wi have to tink out some odder way of hiding de rum, or dem we sure catch me nex time."

"You no can tek pass true somebody yard or some oder road, no mek dem see you?" asked Lorita, plumping the potatoes into the big iron black pot.

"No me chile, dem ah look out fe me and dem would ah certain fin' me, aldo ah might ah risk it, and try mek ah fool dem same time. Ah really might ah try it," said Mr. Watson gazing thoughtfully with half-closed eyes out at his donkey which was browsing on some Spanish Needle near the coffee bushes. "But," he added, "ah not trying it agen, bar dis one time. Ah doan seh ah doan mek some money out ah it, but it too risky, it too risky. You can fool dem Constarb today, an' you can fool dem to-marra, but dem wi catch you sometime. You carn fool dem all de time. So ah only going try dis once more." Lorita gazed with some admiration at her father after this truly profound and philosophic speech and grunted in affirmative approval.

"You right, sah, you really right. Me always ah tink dem going ketch you."

Mr. Watson continued to himself. "Yea, sah, me really mus fool dem dis time, or else not, me wi know Panish Town inside, and learn how fe eat carnmeal. Dem planth'n roas' yet, Lorita?"

ABOUT THREE WEEKS LATER MR. WATSON again took his way down to the plains, and about four o'clock in the afternoon having accomplished a little transaction of his own at a Sugar Estate, was wending his way back home. His donkey was heavily laden with hampers containing stuff of a weighty nature, and in the outskirts of the village near White Bay, he stopped to adjust the hampers and body ropes more easily. He then continued at a brisker rate through the village, past the shops and market, till he approached the gate of the Police Station Yard. Here he slowed down and in an indifferent and leisurely manner, walked past the gate. He had not gone two yards past however, when he was stopped by a shout from the same Constable that had taken charge of his baggage before. "Miser Watson!" Mr. Watson stopped and turned.

"Miser Watson! a word with you sah! Bring you donkey in too!"

Mister Watson led the donkey back and turned within the station yard where he was met by the Constable and the Corporal.

"Marning, Miser Watson!"

"Marnin' Carporal! marning Sargent!"

The Corporal then addressed him. "Sarry fe stop you, Mister Watson but some people ah seh some tings, bout you, dat you ah sell rum widout license, so as it is my jurisdiction and duty, ah wi have to search your hamper, jus' fe prove dem is arlright."

Mr. Watson at this speech, looked at the Corporal, as if he did not understand him, then, stroking his hand on the side of his face, he said slowly:

"Dat I ah sell rum widout a license?" Then after a pause, he led the donkey forward and said gloomily as if overcome by the wickedness of people. "You no can search him."

The two proceeded to search the hampers while Mr. Watson stood silently by with a look of cold impassive dignity on his face. The Constables quickly took off the "cruckcuss bag," or bag of sack-cloth that covered the contents of the hampers. They then saw that each hamper contained two kerosene tins, covered over at the tops with a piece of cloth tied down tightly. They removed one of these pieces of cloth and saw to their disgust nothing but thick "wet sugar" which filled the pan almost to the brim. They tried the other three and found them just the same, full of wet sugar. The Corporal tried to hide his disappointment and disgust under a cloak of outward good humour.

"People will tell lie Miser Watson," said he, "an ah really lose me drink dis time. Pan sugar is really better to trade in dan rum doh, an ah sorry fe hab to trouble you."

Mr. Watson waited in silence till they had tied back the cloth and put in the bags, then he began:—

"Well, Sargent, you hab you duty, and you tink it right, maybe dat you should ah stop an hones' man ina him way, to go hol' him donkey and search him like any common tief slap ina de public. But I doan tink it right." Mr. Watson's voice rose higher, "I' doan tink it right. Seh help me, if ah doan tink you treat me like any common dirty tief dat dem haul go ah Spanish Town. If dat—"

"Go on you way and doan mek a noise in de yard," said the Corporal, angry at his failure to find rum and the hypocritical defence of Mr. Watson. "Go out de yard."

"Ah goin, ah goin!" said Mr. Watson moving out. "You tink ah would ah stay yah in dis place, weh dem mek me out a criminal; an hones man got no place ina dis yard."

With this parting shot Mr. Watson and his donkey took their way out and went again on their journey home. Long after dusk he reached his yard, where he found Lorita anxiously looking out for him.

"As ah no see you come by sunset, an it ah get late" said she, "me seh dem mus' ah really catch you dis time, sah. Me really anxious fe you." She helped him unload the donkey and move the hampers inside the kitchen, then gave the beast a little water and tied her out for the night. Returning to the kitchen she filled her father's plate with bread kind roasted and boiled, yams, cocoas and plantain, the whole flavoured with pork and country pepper.

Mr. Watson made a hearty dinner and during the meal gave an account of his meeting with the Constables, and how he fooled them, to his daughter, who listened with much interest.

"An den, as ah come to de station yard gate, ah tek time walk slower fe mek dem tink ah warn go pass widout dem see me, as if ah no care. De Corporal and de Sargen' tan up inside an watch me dem really not any Corporal and Sargent but so. I call dem—an' as ah could ah get bout one yard pas' de gate, de Coporal cry out loud:

"Miser Watson, Miser Watson, ah warn see you. Bring in you donkey come too ina de yard."

"Well, when ah hear dat ah turn roun' as if suprise, and lead de donkey ina de yard."

"You no feel frighten, sah?" asked Lorita as her father paused to put a big piece of "nager" yam in his mouth. Mr. Watson masticated for a few seconds before answering:

"Well, ah doan seh ah doan feel kine o' funny when ah hear me name call sharp, but of course ah doan mek dem see it, but jus' lead me donkey in quiet, an tell dem marnin'. Well den, dem tek off de baig quick fe true; an as dem see de kerosene tin, dem eye jump, and dem whip off de clort quick as anyting."

Mr. Watson paused again to take in some more food and give power to the climax of his tale.

"An what dem seh when dem see de sugar?" asked Lorita eagerly.

"Dem neber seh scarcely a ting" answered her father, "dem so disappoint. Dem could ah only smile an' look like dem torm fool bud. Dey neber would ah guess in dis word dat rum could ah ina wet sugar ina paccy. But you tink de paccy doan fit de kerosene sweet!"

"Weh you get dem sah?" asked Lorita, "down ah White Bay?"

"No me chile," answered Mr. Watson, "ah get dem higher up de beach, at a place dem call it, Lef River Hole, where dem grow like Premento grow yah almos'. Ah fill dem firs' wid de rum and stop up de hole tight, den put dem in de kerosene tin an' fill up de tin wid de pan sugar. Dem could ah neber fine it out."

Mr. Watson by this time had come to the end of his dinner, and he handed over the plate to Lorita, who washed it and put it up in its place on a shelf with a couple of pans and cracked mugs. Her father who was tired and sleepy then went to bed, Lorita following his example, and they were both soon sleeping, if not the sleep of the just, yet the sleep of undisturbed consciences.

The Red Cock

Chapter I

WHEREVER TWO OR MORE ROADS meet in Jamaica, there is, as is doubtless true for other parts of the world, generally to be found one or more shops. Sometimes the situation is important enough to demand first one shop, then a village, then a town, then perhaps a large city according to the development of the country. Jamaica has not yet got many towns however, and the one shop usually become two or three with a couple of other houses around, and is then called a village. In this state it generally remains, and probably will remain for many more years. Beerthsheba belonged to this class, but it had to show as a sign of some advancement, a Post Office; and the Tax Collector came at his times to receive taxes there. It lay in the southern part of the Parish of Manchester and had roads leading from it to Mandeville and Vere and St. Elizabeth; from which it will be seen that it had a good position.

About four or five years ago it was celebrating with much noise and fervour the 1st of August. Very few, if any of those who celebrated remembered why it was a public holiday, or brought that forward in their enthusiasm; still they were recognizing it with games and sports. About a hundred yards from the shop, in a field which formed a sort of surburban part of the village, the annual Cricket Match between Beerthsheba and Smithfield was going on, and was being played with much spirit. The pitch consisted of a long naked piece of land; all its grass having been rubbed off by continual running upon, and it was very red and very dirty. As the players went too and fro they gradually par took of its redness in their clothes and socks (for most played in their socks alone). It took a lot however to tint the original colours of some of the socks, these being very brilliant in hue—purple, and yellow, and red. These facts did not detract from the enjoyment of the game, and the pitch was certainly more level with the grass off. The spectators, other than the men of the team now batting, were chiefly women and girls selling bread and cakes and ginger beer. The absence of the men was due in a measure to the fact, that there was a game cock fight just about to begin outside the saddler's shop, and there thirty or forty men were collected round two who had a cock each in their hands. Game cock fighting happened now to be very much in vogue, and like all other transitory amusements had a good deal of enthusiasm behind it. The present fight was between Mr. Joe Robinson's "High Licker" and Mr. James Bolton's "Harkaway," and the stakes were £2 a side. These stakes were formed from twenty shares of two shillings each, ten of which had been taken by an owner of one cock, the rest being divided among ten other shareholders. Thus either cock had eleven enthusiastic backers, not counting the interested spectators who indulged in independent bets and shouting. The referees were two shopkeepers, and men of standing, as one could easily perceive from their dress and high dignity of bearing. Among those nearest the cocks, which was long and grave, a shareholder in the company which favoured Mr. Robinson. He took great interest in the proceedings, but did not grow loudly excited as the others did. His name was Mr. William Watson of Every Garden, this being the name of his place. Suddenly the chief shopkeeper raised his hand,—

"Let them fly," said he and the owners raising their birds flung them at one another. Mr. Robinson's bird was smaller than the other, but looked more game to experienced eyes. Either fowl had had its spurs cut off and a sharp long piece of steel substituted, clumsily, in their place to produce a more deadly battle. The cocks now began to spar in earnest and various opinions were passed and good humoured remarks:—

"Hi! Miser Robinson! You fowl good, you know. Him little but h'n trong."

"Come on now, I wi' bet you five poun' dat de red cock beat; yes me son, five poun'!"

"Five poun', Lard me Massa, ah since when Charlie get five poun. H'n mus' ah tief it from old Fader Dennis!"

"Choh no man!" said another, "He mus' a going married to dat yaller giurl from Queentown. I no hear she got money."

"Shut you mout, you impudent chap you!"

"Hi! Miser Watson, ah bet you a sixpence 'gainst you raw-bone jackass dat de yaller cock beat!"

There was some laughter at this, but Mr. Watson disdained to answer. He only scratched his side whisker.

"Hi, de yellow cock ah gie de oder all him looking for! Mises Robinson, I gie you quatty fer you cock!"

"Quatty and gill!" yelled another. Here a shout went up:—"Fus blood, for Miser Bolton Harkaway!"

"Hah, what ah tell you, I know deyaller cock would ah win!"

"Cho, man, him doan win yet You wi soon see him favour John-crow when h'n going dead."

The odds now were in Bolton's favor and the red cock seemed indeed goin to lose, when suddenly he began to attack with fury and jumping up high, came down with a cruel slash across the head of Harkaway, blinding him in one eye. A great shout went up:—

"De red cock beat! De red cock beat!"

"Him doan beat!"

"Him do beat; you no see him wun get up!"

"H'm no beat, ah tell you!"

"Ah wha ah tell you! Han up me sixpence!"

"Han up which sixpence? ah owe you any sixpence!"

"Doan mek ah get angry yah, today! Did you not gie de sixpence you bet wit me to George Bent to hol', and den tek it weh when you see ah going win?"

"Oh man de bet off!"

"De bet off what! you is a d—m wutless scoundrel!"

"Ah who you ah call all de wutless scoundrel? Jus' call me so agen!"

"You *is* a scoundrel!"

The one struck the other and a scuffle ensued. They came apart and took on an awful appearance of most deadly hatred. One feared for their lives.

"Now you jus' strike me agen!"

"Strike you wha! You strike me fus?"

"Jus' strike me! You jus' hit me!"

"Well you jus' hit me fus', and I wi' show you what you want!"

It ended in each requesting the other to hit him, but as the other refused to do such a rude and unchristian act, the quarrel evaporated gradually. During this the yellow cock had fallen, and refused to get up though urged by his owner to do so. The referees then adjudged the victory to Mr. Robinson's High Licker. As soon as the red cock had beaten the other to the ground, it might have been observed that his eleven backers had showed in round the stakes holder, and when victory was declared, hastily took their money from him and also their rival company's. Plenty of vigorous language was being shouted on all sides, as the losers tried to get out their bets and the winners urged their rights. By one of those powerful unwritten laws which hold all the world over, Mr. Robinson had to stand drinks for the defeated company and everybody adjourned to the most popular of the rum shops, which by the way, belonged to one of the referees. Here for two or three hours, plenty of shouting, argument in very curious English, and some quarrelling which ended in words for the most part, went on. The negro does not as a rule need much rum to make him tipsy, for a very little affects him. He seldom however gets really very drunk, or intoxicated to that extent that he cannot go home without help. This is true for the country parts, where the lack of ready money, perhaps has something to do with the soberness of the people. Nearly every shop outside the towns in Jamaica sells rum and other intoxicants, but this does not mean that there is an excess of drinking among individual parties, but rather that nearly everybody takes a drink now and then. After an half hour's convivality, Mr. Robinson who was rather cautious as regards all his money affairs, took his cock and started for home accompanied by his wife and Mr. Watson whose home also lay in the same direction.

"You going home soon," said Mr. Watson, to Mr. Robinson, "You not going join in de spoart at de shop?"

"No sah, no port for me, ah win me money fair, ah wah ah going spen, it for? ah hab one drink, dat's all ah want more?" "Tell me; he added half angrily and half drunkenly to Mr. Watson." "Tell me sah, you tink a man should ha' spen' and wase h'm money pon de ting dem call rum and get drunk like a beas. Dem is a fool."

"You speak true sah," said Mr., Watson soothingly, "Dem is a fool." "But sah, when ah see you fowl beat, ah really glad. Him is de bes' bird bout."

"Him good, him really good," agreed Mr. Robinson, whose ager passed away at once, excessive amiability taking its place.

"Did you see how h'm rise up and slash de oder cross de head? me heart leap till ah tink it going pop, when ah seem gie dat blow.

Mr. Watson eyed the bird with grave admiration. "Wunderful, sah, wunderful" "An' how much" with a diferential air that flattered Mr. Robinson, "would you be askin' for a cock like dat sah?"

Mr. Robinson looked at him as if he did not understand.

"An' how much would ah ask fe him?" he repeated.

"But him not fe sale. You tink ah would ah sell dis fowl; ah woulden sell him, not even if ah ah dead fe hungry, an me belly swell out like dem little maugre pig. Ah bring up dis cock from de berry egg shell, and ah watch him and see him grow to dis size and den ah going sell him?"

"No sah, you don understan me," said Mr. Watson, hastening to pacify the other; "ah don mean to ask you how much you would ah sell him for, but what, jis out of curiousness, you tink him wut? Ah no hear dis man Thomas Simit seh him would ah gie ten shillin' fe him?"

"Ah know, ah know," said Mr. Robinson, "h'm offer me dat already, h'n na sell."

"Me hab a little money from me tobacco and premento," said Mr. Watson musingly, "if ah could get a real good bud like dat, ah would ah buy him. Doh ah mus' seh dem is a risky ting to keep. Dem may boat, and den agen dey may lose an' you no know when dem going sick."

"My fowl na going sick!" said Mr. Robinson as if in protest to some remark against his cock.

From these casual remarks, Mr. Watson gradually led up to the direct question of asking Mr. Robinson to sell him his fowl, and he was in full persuasion when they came to the meeting of the two paths which led from the public road to their respective homes. Finding Mr. Robinson obdurate and quite opposed to any business, Mr. Watson scratched his right whisker philosophically and said goodbye.

"Well as you wun do any business Miser Robinson and ah doan seh you wrong, I mus go me way. Evenin'! sah, evenin'! Miss Ann!" this to Mrs. Robinson who had been walking as a wife should about ten yards behind her husband.

"I wish you a good evenin' sah!"

It was dusk when after a couple of minutes walk from where he had separated from the other two, Mr. Wat on entered his own yard. His daughter a ragged girl of about twelve had preceded him, and had stirred up the fire in the rotten shaky looking kitchen to greater vigour by the addition of some wood. The walls of the kitchen were of plaster white washed outside, but lacking this dressing inside. The inside however, to make up for the coating of white-wash had taken to itself several coatings of soot and was very black and dirty especially near the fire corners. From the rafters of the thatched roof, hung bundles of tobacco leaves which were being cured in an atmosphere of peculiar smell, born of smoke and other odours. It is easy to recognise this smell, when on a pleasant summer evening, a man will pass on the road smoking his "donkey rope." The seat of honour, a polished block of wood, stood near the fire, and around were various odds and ends, old pans, cocoa heads, a donkey's pack saddle, etc. This roomwas Mr. Watson's study, dining hall, pantry and kitchen. When Mr. Watson entered and took his accustomed seat, the girl was stirring a pot of red peas soup, and a little boy of grave long face, inherited doubtless from his father, was sitting in one corner eagerly awaiting his dinner.

"You feed de pig yet Josiah?" asked Mr. Watson of this little boy.

"Yes sah, me feed him dun dis long time,"

"Ah want you go wid me to de groun' tomorrow to help me carry some potatoh slip," said Mr. Watson; "ah doan wan mek de season pass."

"Me have fe go up to Cedar Valley to morrer go bruk premento sah!" said Josiah in his shrill young voice.

"Hi fe true," said Mr. Watson. "I nuh fuhget. You tell Miser Torn dat you wun tek fipence a day?"

"Yes sah, but him seh sah, dat if ah doan wan de fipence, ah fe stay way sah."

Mr. Watson gave a grunt and was silent. The soup was now ready and the girl poured it into three receptacles, a blue soup plate with a yellow border, which as being the only soup plate belonged to Mr. Watson naturally, a cracked mug which the girl kept for herself, and a tin pannikin which the boy eagerly accepted. They had pewter spoons however of the same pattern, design and size. After finishing his soup and some roasted potatoes the boy departed to his bed, which was a sort of bench in the hall of the house proper. On his leaving the kitchen, his father began a conversation with his daughter:—

"Lorita, ah offer Miser Robinson eleven shilling for his cock dis evenin' an he wun tek it."

Lorita who was a thin featured and sharp looking girl looked at her father then laughed. "Him mus a fool."

Mr. Watson fingered the few hairs that formed his right whisker: "You speak true, Lorita h'n is a fool. When a man see eleven shillin' in h'n han' h'n should a sell. You no know when time mongoose goin' tek you fowl or h'n may dead or h'n even walk way."

Mr. Watson then lowered his voice and proceeded to whisper cautiously, "Stop you laughing Lorita and listen to me. Ah been tell all o' dem dis evenin' dat ah goin to me Uncle a Santa Cruz tomorrow, so dey won know. Ah going start ina morning soon an' you mus come down Thursday night (It was now Monday) to de Bay cross roads whey I wi meet you. You certain you know whey fe do? eh? Lorita nodded.

"Ah know fe certain sah, ah could ah walk bout dat yard ina blackes' night."

Well ah speak to you enuf to mek you unerstan an' you ought to do it right. But ah wi tell you over agen.

Mr. Watson kept on whispering loudly and earnestly to Lorita for about half an hour, then both went to bed in their palatial family house.

Chapter II

ON THURSDAY MORNING ABOUT SEVEN o'clock, Mr. Robinson having rubbed the sleepiness out of his eyes by a vigorous application of water to his face,—this was generally as far as the bath went with him—strolled leisurely round to the back of his house to look at his fowl. To his astonishment he found the door of the coop open and its occupant absent; thinking however that his wife had loosed the cock to have a run, he went back to quarrel with her, for he had, given her no permission to do any such thing. He learnt from her, however, that she was innocent of the charge, neither was anyone of his children guilty. His feeling then became one of terror and anxiety, and he and his household looked long and eagerly for the cock. The news spread quickly among the neighbouring yards, that Mr. Robinson's Red Cock was gone, and by about ten o'clock it became apparent that the fowl had been stolen.

Mr. Robinson now was frantic and his language would have been interesting to the thief if he had been around.

"Ah wish to Gawd Awmighty dat ah could ah hol de man dat tief me fowl. Me Gawd, ah would ah kill him! Ah would ah tear h'n inside out. But whah sort o' man dem hab bout yah dat h'n should ah come slap ina me yard ah night and tek out me fowl. De dam blarsted tief!

Having given up all hope that his fowl had strayed, Mr. Robinson put on his coat and set out for the nearest Police Station, which was about four miles away. He took sometime to walk the distance, as he stopped several time to relate the news to sympathizing friends, and give candidly his opinion of the thief's character.

On arriving at the station, he told his story to the Corporal in charge, and gave a minute description of the fowl, leaving out, however, the fact that it was a game cock. The reason for the latter reticence being that game cock fighting was not allowed by the law. The Corporal told him that he would have the description of the cock sent around through the *Police Gazette*, but said that as Mr. Robinson did not suspect anyone in particular, there was nothing much more to be done.

"You certain that you got no suspicion 'gainst any man at all? he asked."

"No sah, me no got any suspicion," answered Mr. Robinson gloomily.

E.A. DODD

"Dem is all a tief." "But if ah hav' fe spen ebery penny ah got, ah wi punish him," he added vindictively. He then tried at the neighbouring shop to find consolation in a couple of glasses of weak rum and water, but the rum only helped to inflame his passions and he returned home very angry and sullen. His way, when coming to his yard, took him very near Mr. Watson's home, and in passing he might have noticed Lorita fast asleep under a banana tree in some coffee bush. He might have noticed too that she looked very tired, but these little things went unseen to his clouded intellect and he certainly would not, even if he *had* noticed her weariness, dreamt of associating it with the absence of his fowl.

About this very time or a little earlier, Mr. Watson and his "raw-bone jackass," Alice, entered the yard of his uncle "Old Father Matney," after a walk from the bottom of the Manchester Hills. Father Matney's yard was some miles south-east of the village of Santa Cruz, and Mr. Watson and his donkey were rather tired, for the road leading up from the Savannas into the Santa Cruz Mountains is a monotonous and wearying climb, over stiff and numerous little hills. When Mr. Watson entered the yard of his uncle (he was supposed by some to be his father), he found the old gentleman asleep under a mango tree with a bible open in his hands. Father Matney had been rather a wild fellow in his younger days, so to make up for lost time, had taken enthusiastically to religion in his old age. At present his inclinations tended toward Seventh Day Adventism, but he had not become a regular convert and his mind was still open to any taking ideas that might come along. He welcomed his nephew cordially and gave him breakfast which his daughter, a good looking woman of a sort of yellow colour, dished up for them. The name of this woman was Eliza Matney, and she had that peculiar yellow colour of skin which is seen chiefly in the people of the Savannas and hot plains of the Southern and South-western parts of the Island.

"You bring anything fe me Willyam?" said Mr. Matney after the donkey had been unloaded and tied out and they were eating their breakfast. Mr. Watson finished swallowing some boiled potato before answering.

"Well sah ah doan bring nutten much, but knowing dat provision is scace down dis way, ah bring you a couple o' yampi an' cocoh.

"Tenk you me son, tenk you." said the old man, "The blessing of de Lord fall pon you, for you tink bout de ole man an you len to de Lord."

Mr. Watson chewed his yam modestly:—

"Well sah, me doan go to Church ofen, an de collection man dem, doan ofen see me money, an ah swear and all de res' o'it, but ah do tink pon me relations sometime."

"Well Willyam," replied the old man who liked yampie, "so far you bad enuf, but when you gie to me, de poor ole man, you lenin' to de Lord, you lenin to de Lord, an de Lord will repay you, for h'n seh so and h'n hab to.

"Ah notice you hab a cock wid you," changing the subject abruptly. "What you goin do wid it?"

"Ah buy it cheap from a man up ah Plowden," answered Willyam, "ah did hav' de money an it so cheap dat ah buy it for a shillin!"

"Shillin?" said Mr. Matney, "It cheap," an a game cock to?"

"You right sah," said Mr. Watson "ah game cock, an because ah game cock ah buy it. I bring him fe try a fight wid de cock bout yah.

"Cock fightn Willyam?" said Mr. Matney, you going in fe dat, you wi lose money, an' besides its sinful. Aldo you is a young man an you mus hab you way. When you is my age, well den you wi tink more about gettin you soul ready for de great day. But me no hear dat dem doan allow it by law. Dat dem can punish you.

"Dem doan allow it fe true!" agreed Mr. Watson, But if dem doan know, how can dey punish you?"

"Well de station is far enuf away," said Mr. Matney, "an ah doan suppose dey wi catch you. But dese tings is sinful, Willyam! Bery sinful."

Mr. Watson did not think it worth while to take up the question of its sinfulness, and went on eating without making a reply. However, Mr. Matney finding his nephew unwilling to discuss cock fighting from a religious point of view, limited himself to the financial and social sides of the sport. For an old man who was supposed to be wrapped up in the pursuit of religion, he showed a surprisingly keen knowledge of his neighbours affairs, what sort of cocks they had, and the latest fights that had come off.

"It really curious, Willyam," remarked Mr. Matney, "dat as you comin' to see me you should a buy a game cock, an you no know dat dem ah fight cock up yab. It really curious."

"You speak true sah"; said Mr. Watson gravely, "it really curious."

"All tings is in the han of de Lord" said Mr. Matney without intending any irreverence.

Mr. Watson learnt from Matney and Eliza that a certain Philip Brown living two miles away, had a cock that had beaten nearly every other cock in the district. It would be easy to get up a fight between the two cocks, for Brown was keen on the sport and had won plenty of money on his. Mr. Matney seemed doubtful about the advisability of fighting such a good cock without trying theirs first, but Mr. Watson assured him that his cock was quite capable of beating any cock around, and he was going to Mr. Brown's in the morning to arrange the combat.

Next morning Mr. Watson found Mr. Brown quite willing to have the fight, and it was arranged that a duel, with a bet of ten shillings a side, should come off at Ole Matney's yard between the two cocks that day.

At noon then of the next day, Mr. Brown with his fowl and small party of backers went to Mr. Matney's yard where they found awaiting them, Mr. Watson with his fowl and his backers. After a few preliminaries such as placing the stakes in the hands of some worthy man and appointing two judges, a ring was formed round Mr. Watson and Mr. Brown and the fight began. During the fight a man who had but lately come from Manchester was struck with the resemblance between Mr. Watson's cock and a fowl, which he said belong to one Mr. Robinson who lived near Beersheba. "Ah neber see two fowl favour so"; said he, "Aldo ah do see a difference. But dem do favour fe true."

"You right, Marse John," said Mr. Watson heartily, "Ah know Miser Robinson fowl eben more dan ah know dis, an ah neber see such a likeness. Same so de oder one red!"

"De berry same!" said Marse John, "only fe you cock little smaller!"

"Ah tink so meself" agreed Mr. Watson, "Him little smaller."

The fight took place with less noise than at Beersheba, but it was longer and more game. After about ten minutes, severe sparring however, Mr. Watson's red cock first wounded and then completely de feated the other and his owner was richer by ten shillings.

After the shouting had stopped and some hostile arguments had passed off, Mr. Watson and Mr. Matney brought out some glasses, some rum and some water; and everybody had a drink in the red cock's honour. Mr. Matney, who had a strong belief in the idea that all things little or great that profited him, were the work of Providence, and that anything that was unfortunate was the work of Satan, was especially joyful and even took a drop of rum in excess of good fellowship. Mr. Brown and his party finally took their departure about an hour later, taking with them however, an open challenge to anybody in the district, who having a cock might like to fight.

As the result of this challenge, no less than four fights came off during then ext two or three weeks, of which Mr. Watson's cock won three, and his Master we will not say owner—gained £2 in all. It is to be feared that Mr. Matney's soul did not benefit by Mr. Watson's stay, and he had, for several lapses in sinfulness, to make up by many outward signs of remorse and much bible reading.

At the end of the third week however, Mr. Watson sent Eliza Matney's little boy to Lorita at Every Garden with some tobacco and a message, and two days after the boy had come back, he departed himself from his uncle's yard. He went away at an exceedingly early hour of the morning, near midnight in fact, and by some strange coincidence met Lorita at the foot of the Manchester hills on his way to Alligator Pond at about two o'clock in the morning. Lorita did not stop to talk, however, but started off back home at a very quick walk, while her father went on in a leisurely manner to the bay. Two days later he returned home and found all the neighbourhood excited over the curious way in which Mr. Robinson's red cock had come back to his coop after a disappearance of three weeks about. Mr. Robinson himself did not know what to make of it, and meeting Mr. Watson on the day of the latter's return, expressed his opinions:—"Well Miser Watson, such a ting sah! Fus' ah lose him an ah sure somebody tief him, and den when ah ah look after to fin' de tief, de fowl come back. De only ting sah, is dat eider some man tief it an' put it back because h'm frighten o' me, or dat it some o' dem blarsted obeahman tricks."

Mr. Watson stroked his whisker thoughtfully:—"Well den ah doan tink it's obeahman Miser Robinson, from what I understan; but rader dat it's some tief, who mus' ah tek it weh and as you seh, h'm so frighten dat it put h'n back. But dayse wickedness sah!"

The Courting of the Dudes

Chapter I

"Heh, heh, heh eh. . .! Doan bodder me son! But coo Thomas nuh! But Lar! dayse trouzez and de gaiters—jus ah boasy! You ah go courting, nuh Thomas?"

Thomas for answer made a quick grab at the small barefooted boy who thus impertinently addressed him; failing to hold him however as the latter had been expecting the grab and easily escaped. Thomas in the glory of Sunday clothes did not think it worth while to go after him so merely remarked in tones that were not very vindictive:—

"Alright Hezekiah, you jus' wait yah till ah come back from chutch! Ah gie you arl you looking for. You too bloomin' farce."

Hezekiah at this merely laughed a shrill young laugh and followed his brother out of the yard,—at a respectable distance however. Thomas's get up was certainly one to evoke attention if not admiration in all other people. His shoes beginning from the bottom were of the fashionable colour brown, and of a peculiar and stylish cut, being a sort of cross between a shoe and boot. They were not high, nor yet low, buttoned by two rows of four buttons each, yet also laced with broad brown laces. Just above the shoes, sufficiently high to give a glimpse of a purple sock, came the end of a remarkably fine pair of light coloured gaiters, tailor made of corduroy and fastened with large buttons. The light colour of the gaiters was in fine contrast to a pair of dark brown trousers, which appeared also to advantage against the brilliant hues of a sash which looked like silk, but which, it was to be feared, was only coloured cotton or cretonne. Above this encincture shone out in dazzling splendour a full expanse of white shirt, with silver studs all complete. The coat which bounded this snowy bosom, was of a bright blue shade with a large handkerchief hanging half-way out of the breast pocket, hiding the end of a silver chain which passed from the first button hole and had several large and ornate charms hanging to it. His hat, a new stylish felt, bought only a week ago, rested lightly on the "brush top" of his head, which was held a little stiffly by a high collar girt, at its base by a red and green necktie. The tie was kept well in place by a necktie clip of ornate and chaste design, bought of a Syrian peddlar. As jewelry, other than the charms of his watch chain, Thomas had two silver rings on a little finger, one of which had its value enhanced by a large red stone cut like a seal. He carried an orange stick or rather cane nicely varnished in his hand, and had as a finishing touch to a masterly and most effective get-up, a gorgeous ginger lily in his button hole. Thomas was undoubtedly *the* Dude of the district.

They,—for Hezekiah was also going to church and was also dressed in Sunday clothes, which unlike those of his brother consisted simply of a blue suit and cap,—proceeded along in silence following a path which led over a stone wall into the pasture of a property or pen, through this pasture then over another stonewall and into the public road. Thomas did not walk too quickly for the day was warm, and the heat might take a bit of the polish off his appearance. To prevent any risk however to his collar, he stuffed his handkerchief round his neck between the skin and collar during his journey through the pasture; coming out on the highway he removed the handkerchief back again into its former elegant position.

As he and Hezekiah came into the road the first person they met was Mr. George Green, a teacher, riding on a young and rather small horse. Teachers in Jamaica generally ride, and it is strange how one can easily single one of that class from a crowd without any foreknowledge that he be a teacher. There is a mixed air of respectability, some bumptiousness, some self-assurance, some timidity, some importance, that always gives them away. Mr. Green in his way, was also a bit of a dude, not so flashy or bright as Thomas, but as befitted a older man and a teacher, more given to dress that showed solidity and dignity in its foundations. On this occasion he sported a pair of leather leggings, black and shiny, a rather dark suit with its coat cut long, and a collar, the lowness of which was due to the thickness and shortness of the neck it encircled.

Mr. Green greeted them with an affable and slightly condescending smile:—"Good morning Thomas! morning Hezekiah!"

Thomas answered with a rather absent-minded "mornin' sah!" for the sight of Mr. Green riding so stylishly and with such dignity to church had set him thinking about his chances in love against such a rival, for be it known, Thomas and the teacher were rivals for the hand of fair (meaning comely) Miss Annabel Gibson who could not make up her mind which to choose. Thomas had the advantage of seeing her, far more often than Mr. Green whose duties kept him busy, and although up to now she had seemed gracious to him, still she had not refused altogether the advances of the other, and the position and comfortable salary of the teacher often obtruded themselves on his mind and made him gloomy. For some little way along the road his mind was thus melancholy, but the cheerful salutations of aquaintances that he met bound for church, added to the brightness of the morning, gradually dispelled his gloom, and by the time the church had come in sight round a corner of the road, he was feeling quite good-humoured. Besides was he not going to have the privilege of walking home with Miss Annabel after church!

Mr. Green had gone on ahead, presenting by the help of a martingale as well as a curb and snaffle bit on the mouth of the horse, a stylish and spirited appearance.

When Thomas had walked through the gates of the church yard, past the church and up to the school house he found Mr. Green talking to Miss Annabel, and her mother Mrs. Gibson under a mango tree.

He was neither surprised nor dismayed however, for he felt that off his horse the teacher was not such a terrible foe, so he took off his hat gracefully and shook hands rather bashfully with Mrs. Gibson and Miss Annabel. Mrs. Gibson who was dressed in a much starched print gown that stuck out around in stiff folds, accorded him a kindly "How you do dis morning Thomas?" and Miss Annabel who looked charming in a white dress trimmed with bright blue ribbons and girt at the waist with a belt, also of a blue ribbon, gave him a gracious "mornin' Thomas." Thomas felt that he had not got himself up for nothing.

As they had a few minutes to wait before the service would begin, they remained under the mango tree for the time chatting; or rather the teacher and Mrs. Gibson chatted, the younger two being self-conscious were silent enough.

"How is Mr. Gibson? asked Mr. Green of Miss Gibson. "I doun see him in attendant anywhere." "No sah," answered Mrs. Gibson, "H'n not yah today; H'n not feeling too well dis morning; H'n nuh really what you would ah call sick, but jus' enuf to no mek him warn go a church."

"Perhaps doh," said the teacher looking about him, "The mornin' is so bright and warm, it might have do him good—Been effecatious."

"You speak true sah. It might ha ha really do him good," said Mrs. Gibson, "but h'n jus 'tan so but h'n doan feel incline."

"Well however, de family well represent" said Mr. Green gallantly, an Miss Ann look so agreeable dis mornin'.

At this Mrs. Gibson said, "Hi Misar Green!" while Miss Ann turned her head away with a bashful giggle. Thomas did not appreciate the teacher's compliments but he made the best of it and grinned too.

The bell-ringing had now come to a stop so they all went into the church to take their seats, being joined at the door by Annabel's sister, Susan, who had been talking to someother people.

The Gibsons occupied a pew on the gallery upstairs, and Thomas took a seat in a pew not far off, but the teacher being a man of some consequence in the church had a seat downstairs in the body of the church.

The service went on as most services do in the country parts, with plenty of late arrivals coming in every now and then. The young men and young women in Jamaica of the lower class do not consider that boots are worth anything in style or appearance unless they (the boots) creak exceedingly loudly, so the reason of any young man coming in late is probably to show off his clothes and boots.

After service, Thomas and the two Miss Gibsons stayed in for Sunday School which of course Mr. Green attended, being indeed one of the class instructors. When the Sunday School had finished, Thomas and the two girls started for the Gibsons' residence, Mr. Green having first bidden farewell, squeezing Miss Annabel's hand tenderly on the act.

The three walked along the road back, the way Thomas came, for the girls' house lay in somewhat the same direction as Thomas', save that they would not go through the pasture.

The order and manner in which Thomas and the girls walked home was rather peculiar and not to appearances and foreign eyes, the most sociable. Instead of the three walking side by side, they walked separately; Thomas keeping to one side of the road and the two girls to the other. The girls did most of the talking and giggling, though Thomas every now and then would break in with a facetious remark from across the road. They reached Mr. Gibson's place after what seemed a short walk to Thomas, and had a cheerful lunch of bread and sugar and water. Then Thomas went home feeling somewhat satisfied, but not entirely so.

Chapter II

ON THE WEDNESDAY AFTER THE Sunday Miss Annabel received two letters from the Post Office at Beersheba. She did not open them at once, because it so happened that though she was a well brought up girl, she was unable to read, and she wanted the addresses read out in all their importance first. Her sister Susan who also could not read was as much excited over them as herself, and the two giggled and guessed to their hearts-content. It is not impossible that both knew intuitively whom the epistles came from.

However, during the middle of the day they went over to the neighbouring yard of a certain Mr. Richard Timsin a kind hearted man, who having had a much better education in his youth than those of his rank, was looked upon as the scholar of the district, and usually called upon to transact any literary business, such as letter-reading and letter writing of his neighbours. This Mr. Timson was rather a character in his way. As a boy and young man he went to the Mico in Kingston, and after that took up teaching on his own account. Not finding this to pay, however, he went to Colon and was also in the stoker line on board a ship for a short time. After a time when only about thirty years of age he got tired of moving about and returned to his home in the country and took up life again as a labourer and settler. He had a higher sense of honour than possessed by his fellows, and was kind-hearted and cute, though a bit of a rogue.

Mr. Timson had just finished his breakfast when the girls entered the yard, and was sitting with his back against his kitchen wall picking his teeth.

"Mornin' Miser Timsin,!" said the girls approaching. "Mornin' Miss Ann! Mornin' Miss Sue!" answered Mr. Timsin pleasantly. You come to see me? "Yes sah!" answered Ann shyly, "Me come fe ask if you could ah read two letter fe me; dat ah get dis mornin'."

"Ah love letter?" asked Mr. Timsin looking up at them with a smile.

"Me no know sah!" answered Ann with a giggle. "How me fe know what kind o' letter dey is, if ah doun read dem."

"Where de letter?" asked Mr. Timson.

Ann produced them and gave them to him. Mr. Timson looked at them with interest. The addresses were in widely different styles of hard writing. One was written in a quick ornate manner, with large flowing capitals and plenty of flourishes; the other in a small manner with very little flourish. Mr. Timson read out both addresses carefully and slowly, though they were just the same:—

Miss Annabel Gibson,
Happy Home,
Beersheba P.O.

Finishing the reading he rose; "Come chile, mek we go in the Hall. Love letter not fe read out a doors!" So saying he entered the Hall which with the bedroom made the House, followed by the girls He took a seat in a stiff home-made mahogany chair and gave the girls a bench. Having put on his spectacles as necessary part of the insignia of a scholar, Mr. Timson opened the letter with the large ornate writing and began to read out slowly and carefully:—

Beersheba School,
12 Aug. 1900—

Dear Annabel,

    As I take up my pen to write you these lines, I feel inmesurably the limitation of the body, which cannot express what my heart feels for you. Do you love me? If so tell me quickly that my mind might rest—for I cannot sleep night or day—my mind is so fix on you. I would like to see you face to face that I might have then throw off the burden if I know you love me. Will you be at the Picnic at White Hall on Saturday? I will be there and hope to see your dear face and hear that you love me. I hope your father is recovered, and that you are well. You do not know how my whole mind and physic."

    When Mr. Timsin got to "physic" he stopped. Physic! Physic!" he said thoughtfully," what you mean? De man ah talk bout him Physic as if hn ah tek medicine. You know what him mean Miss Ann? Miss Ann twisted her handkerchief:—"Me no know sah."

    Mr. Timsin read it out again; "Physic! But stop!" it suddenly dawned on him, "oh fe true, him mean physique, which means de body or constitution. You understand?" The girls nodded and he went on. "You do not know how my whole mind and physique fix on you, and my spirit is crying for you. *Do, do* come to me. I am coming to a close. Give my best regards to your parents, and please accept 100 kisses from me, who is and always will be

Your loving and dear well wisher,
George Green

    "Well, Miss Ann" said Mr. Timsin, looking at the letter as he finished. "Dat ah proper love letter! You going tek him?"

Miss Ann held out her hand for the letter:—

"H'n too foolish!" said she. "Tenk you sah, Gimme dat and read de oder."

Mr. Timsin handed her the letter and opening the other unfolded the sheet and read as follows:—

Lang Syne
13 Aug., 1900

Dear Ann,

When I was with you on Sunday, I meant to have tell you of my love for you, but when it come to the front all courage leave me. How weak we are in the presence of that whom we love! How can I make you know how much I love you? From when we was young and going to school I love you up to now. Sometime I think you love me a little, and then again my heart ready to sink. Tell me darling, do you love me. The ring is round and has no end, so is my love for you. Are you going to the Picnic at White Bay on Saturday? I shall be there (D. V.), and shall get my answer from your dear mouth. I cannot stay here if you don't love me, so please don't send me away. Give my regards to your mother and father and receive my love and kisses.

Your loving one,
Thos. Bonito

Mr. Timsin read out the name of the writer with a kind of pompous flourish, then looked at the letter again as if admiring the writing. "Well, ah doan know how you feel, Miss Ann," he said, after a little pause, "but I like dis letter better than the other. But it not my business. Which one you going tek?" he asked with a smile.

"Tek wha?" answered Miss Ann loudly "me going tek any o' dem? Dem too fool. Weh me got fe do wid love letter and such ting. Gimme de letter sah?" Hereupon Miss Ann began to laugh and giggle, which showed she was rather pleased to receive two love letters.

"Well it not my business"; said Mr. Timsin giving her the letter, "but to tell you the truth and I can deny it, if I was you I would ah tek Thomas, ah know him from a chile and you know him too an' h'n would ah suit you bes. But of course you wi please youself and ih not my business."

"Me like Thomas better meself"; said Susan. "De teacher too high an' mighty fe me."

Ann was silent and gave no opinion, simply tugged at her dress and laughed. After a little she rose. "Come Susan!" said she, "mek me goh." Turning to Mr. Timsin, "me tenk you sah fe read de letter. It really kind o' you."

"Oh, no trouble at all," said Mr. Timsen, "me always like fe read love letter, an of course I'm not the wan to say anything 'bout them."

"Tenk you sah," said Ann gratefully moving with Susan out through the door.

As they went into the yard Mr. Timsin shouted after them. Miss Ann, you going to the Picnic?"

"Me na know sah": answered back Miss Ann. "Dem too foolish."

Mr. Timsin smiled at the answer as he sat in his chair, and it was really a charming smile so full of kindliness, good humour and wisdom.

"Ah well," he muttered to himself with a sigh as he rose.

"Dem is young. I hope she wi tek Thomas." But he added, "Ah really write that letter of Thomas well. De teacher nowhere with me."

SATURDAY THE DAY OF THE Picnic broke cloudless and exceeding fair, and for its appointed time kept bright and warm with the bright warmness that the black man loves. Everybody was in good spirits, and Mr. Honeyman who was giving the picnic seemed to be going to get a lot of money. The picnic entrance fee for grownups 6d., for children 3d., had been advertised all around and promised to be a success, for by three o'clock, an hour after it opened, plenty of people were on the grounds, which had been lent by the owner of White Hall to Mr. Honeyman. The sports had now commenced, for be it known, a picnic is not a picnic without the sports. These sports generally consisted of Foot Races, Obstacle Races, Jumping, High Jump and Low Jump, sometimes Horse Races, and other interesting and manly events. You pay a small entrance fee, and if you win the race or event, you get a prize provided by the giver of the picnic.

In this picnic of Mr. Honeyman's there were quite a number of events and the prizes were such as to excite intense desire aud envy of the young men and women, for of course there were a couple of events for girls, races, etc. The prizes were of great variety, White Shirts, Coloured Shirts, Belts, Watches, Knives, Needle Cases etc.; but the prize was undoubtedly a pig, a live pig; and the event for which the pig was prize was the most interesting and exciting, and yet most simple. All one had to do was to pay a sixpence for entering, then try and catch the pig by its greased tail; the first person that caught it properly and firmly got the pig.

At half past three the Gibsons arrived, and were met at the gate by Thomas who insisted on paying for Susan and Ann's tickets, so gaining a point from the teacher who had not arrived yet. Miss Ann who looked even more charming than usual, gave Thomas a shy smile that might have meant anything. As a matter of fact Miss Ann had not made up her mind yet which to take. She liked Thomas much better than the teacher, but the latter's dignity of position and comfortable circumstances still influenced her mind. Thomas who was going to partake in some of the sports, had left his gaiters at home, and was now wearing brilliant blue stockings, with brown shoes. The three passed through the gate, into the grounds and stood up watching a foot race which was being run. Just as the race was ended in a tremendous burst of cheers and noise, Mr. Green rode up to them looking most important and affable on his young and small horse which was prancing and curvetting in a stylish way. When he saw Thomas with the girls, his face darkened a little, but it cleared almost at once, and dismounting he was gallant graciousness itself. "I am very glad you have managed to come and shed your pleasant influence on the scene today Miss Ann! said he, I don't know how I come so late. The reports of the school that I was writing, bas delayed me."

The next foot race was one in which Thomas was going in for, so he left Ann and Susan in Mr. Green's charge and went off to do his best. During the race, Mr. Green carried off the girls to have ice cream and cakes, and when Thomas amidst tremendous clamour won the race, and a watch at the same time, the girls were absent eating their cakes. Putting on his shoes again he took the watch, and after a little looking, found them. Mr. Green received him with a condescending and affable smile. "I am glad you have obtained the victory Thomas!" and Ann said shyly.

"Ah glad you win Thomas" and asked to see the watch. Thomas was more than proud.

"You deserve a drink for that race": said Mr. Green. "What will you tek, a syrup or a kola?"

Thomas who did not see why he should not benefit at the teacher's expense, answered readily:—

"Me tink me wi tek a kola, tank you sah!"

Mr. Green ordered a kola and Thomas drunk it off one breath.

When the girls had finished their ice cream and cakes, Mr. Green paid up, rattling the loose money in his pocket incidentally as he put his hand in, and they all went out to see and enjoy what was going on. "You na going in for de next race Sue" asked Thomas.

Susan nodded, "Yes, Me believe me going. Ah really tink ah might ah try."

"You doan bring you entrance money yet?" said Thomas.

"No said Susan, "me doan bring it yet."

"Dats alright den," said Thomas, "I wi pay fe it."

"Tenk you Thomas," said Susan. "It kine o' you an' ah mus' really try fe win."

So when the next race came on, Susan having her entrance money paid, took her place with the other girls, to run. The distance to run was shorter than that for the boys and men And the girls did almost as quick running as the men. Urged on by Thomas and Ann's shouts, Susan ran as hard as she could but she was a little short-winded and only come in third. She got a small prize however, so she was not much disappointed.

"You warn fe eat less," said Ann, with a sister's frankness, "you too stout."

"Too stout wha?' said Susan, "as ah jus' going win, me breat kine o fail me and I have fe go slower mek ah only get third."

Several interesting events then took place and all were enjoying themselves. At about half-past four Mr. Honeyman announced in a loud voice that the pig race would now come off, and would everybody join in please—only 6d an entry.

After some hesitation several young men entered, including Thomas who saw in the pig perhaps an addition to the property he might possess with Ann.

When Mr. Honeyman had got ten entries and no more seem to be coming, he cleared the ground and prepared to let go the pig. First of all however, he placed the ten young men in a line, and at a distance of ten yards at right angles to opposite the middle man, he placed the pig. Mr. Green who stood near the man and near the pig was to give the signal. Everybody and everything was ready, so lifting up his hand, Mr. Green said, "one! two! three!" and dropped a handkerchief. Immediately Mr. Honeyman let go the pig and immediately the young men started after it. The pig was not exactly fat and rather in good training being lean and muscular, and long and narrow, with a well greased tail. Now the fun and excitement began. The pig first of all, ran away from the men, then being headed, ran this way and that. One or two grabbed the tail, but couldn't grasp it firmly, and away the pig bolted, in and out among the spectators. Here and there it ran, twisting this way and that, squealing and causing some tumbles as people jumped and got out of the way. Thomas kept well after the pig, but did not try after its tail, knowing that it would be too greasy at first. After about five minutes of intense enjoyment to the crowd, the thing happened which finally decided Miss Ann in her choice of husband and gave Thomas a pig and a wife. The pig had come by this time round to its original position and was getting a little bit tired and going slower, was hard pressed indeed, for three young men were almost on him. Now it must be mentioned that just near here there was a large stone with a small piece of naked and dirty land, at the edge of which the teacher was standing and looking on with a dignified smile. As the foremost of the young men started forward to grab, the pig, with a last despairing effort, made a bolt to right angles and ran by Mr. Green. Mr. Green in getting out of the way stumbled against the stone and fell heavily on the pig and in the red and dirty patch of ground. At tremendous shout of cheers and laughter went up, especially magnified when it was seen that Thomas taking advantage of the pig being nearly squeezed to death by the teacher, had grabbed the tail firmly and in fact had won the prize. Mr. Green slowly rose to his feet, covered with red dust, all over his face and shirt. He began to smile in a sickly way at first, but as he heard the shouts and laughter on all sides, his face got darker and darker. The black race loves a joke like this.

"Hi, Miser Green, you mus' ah sorry you no enter fur de race. You would ah get de pig," yelled one.

"Hi, no man!" said another, "De pig get him." Everybody was laughing and shouting, including Susan and Ann who shook with enjoyment of the joke. At the moment that the teacher went down, strange to say, Ann knew that she would accept Thomas and could never the teacher. Mr. Green must have felt something of this, for he walked past them without speaking, in a violent rage, and mounting his horse, rode home. Ann saw him go without any regret and it was a beautiful smile that lit her comely black face, when Thomas came up later to receive her words of congratulation.

A Note About the Author

E.A. Dodd is the author of *Maroon Medicine* (1905), a collection of short stories on working class life in Jamaica. Originally written under the pseudonym E. Snod, the collection appeared as part of a series of novellas and short stories published by the *All Jamaica Library*, an influential press established in 1903 by Jamaican poet, novelist, and editor Thomas MacDermot.

A Note from the Publisher

Spanning many genres, from non-fiction essays to literature classics to children's books and lyric poetry, Mint Edition books showcase the master works of our time in a modern new package. The text is freshly typeset, is clean and easy to read, and features a new note about the author in each volume. Many books also include exclusive new introductory material. Every book boasts a striking new cover, which makes it as appropriate for collecting as it is for gift giving. Mint Edition books are only printed when a reader orders them, so natural resources are not wasted. We're proud that our books are never manufactured in excess and exist only in the exact quantity they need to be read and enjoyed.

Discover more of your favorite classics with Bookfinity™.

- Track your reading with custom book lists.
- Get great book recommendations for your personalized Reader Type.
- Add reviews for your favorite books.
- AND MUCH MORE!

Visit **bookfinity.com** and take the fun Reader Type quiz to get started.

Enjoy our classic and modern companion pairings!

Bookfinity is a registered trademark of Ingram Book Group LLC. © 2023 Bookfinity. All rights reserved.

www.ingramcontent.com/pod-product-compliance
Lightning Source LLC
Chambersburg PA
CBHW020605130626
46552CB00007B/3055